Llama Drama

by Julie Dalton

Illustrated by Gregg Schigiel

SCHOLASTIC INC.

New York   Toronto   London   Auckland   Sydney
Mexico City   New Delhi   Hong Kong   Buenos Aires

Published by Scholastic Inc.,
90 Old Sherman Turnpike, Danbury, Connecticut 06816.

SCHOLASTIC and associated logos are trademarks
and/or registered trademarks of Scholastic Inc.

ISBN 0-439-56273-2

First Scholastic Printing, November 2003

Chapters

LLAMA

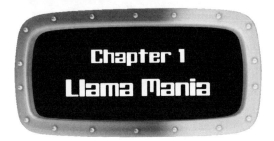

"There, it's finished!" said Jimmy Neutron. He stepped back from his lab table and pointed to a strange-looking device. "Friends, I give you—the Transformatron 4000.

The Transformatron 4000 will revolutionize science," Jimmy continued. "This state-of-the-art machine allows humans to experience firsthand what it's like to be another species. With this, I can temporarily transform any human into any animal. Now I just need a subject to test it out."

"Oh, Jimmy, pick me!" begged his friend
Sheen. "I want to be Ultra Lord.
Pul-eeeeease?"

"No can do, good buddy," responded Jimmy. "The Transformatron 4000 only works with animals, not action figures. But you just gave me an idea for next week's project. In the meantime, I need someone who wants to be an animal."

Jimmy and Sheen turned and looked at their friend Carl.

Carl looked up from his *Llamas Monthly* magazine. "Why are you looking at me? Oh no, Jimmy. Not me this time.

Remember when I tested your self-washing pants?"

"C'mon, Carl," pleaded Jimmy. "You love llamas. It will only be for a few minutes."

But Carl wasn't convinced.

"Picture this," Jimmy argued, "you're standing in front of the class, presenting 'My Life as a Llama.' Why, you would set a new standard for oral reports for all eternity!"

"Er, well . . . ," Carl began.

"I knew you'd say yes!" Jimmy said. "Let's go to the zoo."

The closer the boys got to the zoo, the more nervous Carl became.

"I-I-I'm not sure about this, Jimmy," said Carl. "Will I be home in time for dinner?"

"Goddard: the 3-hour power pack, please," Jimmy told his robot-dog when they reached the llama pen. "I don't want to take

LLAMA

20

any chances. If the Transformatron 4000
runs out of power before I change Carl back,
he'll be stuck as a llama forever."

"C'mon, Sheen, push!" groaned Jimmy.
He and Sheen heaved Carl over the fence
into the pen.

"Now go put your arm around one of the llamas," Jimmy told Carl. "You have to be touching the subject for the Particle Reassignment Beam to work."

"H-h-hi guys," Carl greeted the llamas nervously.

Carl slowly reached out and touched a llama.
Jimmy pushed the button. There was a *hiss*,
a *pop*, and a loud *dingdong*.

Carl turned into a
llama.

Carl the Llama looked happy. But the
other llamas did not. They didn't like
having a stranger in their pen.

In fact, the other llamas began bumping into Carl the Llama and spitting on him. Suddenly one very large wad of spit sailed across the pen and landed on the Transformatron 4000.

FIIZZZTT!!

"Oh no!" cried Jimmy. "The spit from the llama fried the circuits!"

Chapter 3
Showbiz

"Gosh, Jimmy, what's going to happen to Carl?" Sheen asked worriedly. Then he thought for a moment. "Do you think he can get us free passes to the zoo?"

Jimmy was lost in thought. "I have to go back to my lab to fix this. Sheen, you stay here and keep an eye on Carl. I'll be back in a flash."

"Okay, Jimmy," agreed Sheen.

Back in his laboratory, Jimmy carefully opened the Transformatron 4000. "If I can just remove this circuit panel and replace it with a new one . . . ," he muttered. "Now where did I put those extra panels?"

Goddard assisted Jimmy in each step of the process. It took awhile, but the Transformatron 4000 was soon fixed.

To save time, Jimmy drove his hovercraft back to the zoo.

Jimmy landed his hovercraft
in front of the llama pen and
jumped out. Sheen was there
playing with his Ultra Lord.

"I'm back, Sheen. Did anything hap—?"
Jimmy didn't see Carl the Llama anywhere.
"Where's Carl?"

Sheen looked up. "Huh? I dunno. Some guys bought him and took him away."

"Took him away?!" Jimmy shouted. "What do you mean?"

"Well, these two guys drove up in a bus and asked me about Carl," Sheen explained. "I told them he was my friend. They said that Carl should be in showbiz. He could be a star. And Carl seemed to like the idea. Plus those other llamas weren't being so nice to him, so—"

"Shee-een!" Jimmy screamed. "We have to find Carl and change him back! We don't have much time. Think, Sheen! Do you have any idea where they took him?"

"Well, the guys gave me two tickets to this magic show," said Sheen, holding out the tickets. "It's not an Ultra Lord show, but it could be pretty awesome."

"Four o'clock!" Jimmy yelled, looking at his watch. "The show has already started." He jumped into his hovercraft. "C'mon, Sheen! We're going to that magic show to find Carl."

SECTION A
ROW 1
SEAT 6

ONE SHOW ONL
IGMAR & BOB
MAGIC & MYS
SHOWTIME @ 4:

SECTION A
ROW 1
SEAT 7

IGMA
MAGIC &
SHOWTIME

Moments later, Jimmy and Sheen were
pulling up in front of the Retroville
Civic Center.

"Yikes!" Jimmy shouted. "Carl has been a llama for almost 3 hours. If I don't zap him soon, I'll never be able to turn him back."

ROVILLE
CIVIC CENTER

The boys raced into the Igmar and Bob magic show, which was almost over.

"The seats are down front," Jimmy said, pointing. "Maybe we can see Carl."

Sheen couldn't take his eyes off the stage.

Wow!" Sheen cried. "Did you see Ignar and Bob saw that guy in half and then put him back together? I'll bet they would know how to change Carl back into a boy!"

Jimmy sighed and rolled his eyes.

Just then Igmar's amplified voice thundered through the theater. "Ladies und gentlepeople, brrrrace yourselves for ze grand finale!"

With a pop, all the lights went out. A drumroll rumbled, and a spotlight snapped on. There, in the middle of the stage, was a frightened Carl the Llama.

"Oh no!" exclaimed Jimmy. "What have I done?"

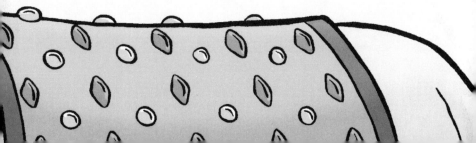

Above where Carl the Llama stood was a disk filled with knives—all pointing down at him.

"Look at the eyes on that animal!" shouted a woman sitting behind Jimmy and Sheen.

"They're so expressive—so human!" agreed her friend.

Igmar's voice boomed, "Dirrrrect your attention to zis gentle crrreature. He is about to take part in a never-before-attempted shtunt. Dangerous? Yessss! Is this adorable llama DOOMED?"

"Wow, Carl is going to get skewered!" Sheen hissed under his breath.

Jimmy looked from Carl the Llama to his watch. "It's now or never," he murmured. Quickly he pulled out the Transformatron 4000 and aimed. "I hope I'm close enough.

There's only enough power to zap once," Jimmy said as he pushed the button on the Transformatron 4000.

Everyone in the audience jumped as fireworks exploded onstage. The lights flashed.

"Wow!" Sheen shouted. "Your Trans-whatchama-thingy really works! Do it again, Jimmy!"

When the smoke cleared, the audience saw that the knife-filled disk had crashed to the floor. Carl the Llama was nowhere in sight.

The audience gasped.

Quickly Igmar and Bob draped the fallen disk with a silky, blue cloth. They raised their arms, then dropped them.

BOOM! sounded another explosion with more fireworks and flashing lights. This time, when the smoke cleared, there on the stage on top of the blue cloth stood . . .

. . . a very confused Carl.

The audience went wild! Everyone was cheering and clapping. "Amazing!" they exclaimed to one another. "How did Igmar and Bob turn that llama into a boy?"

The magicians looked confused at first, but then they bowed and waved.

As soon as the show ended, Jimmy and Sheen raced backstage.

Igmar and
Bob were heroes! No
one could figure out how
they had performed such an
astounding stunt. The magicians
weren't sure themselves, but they knew
they needed Carl. So they begged him to
join their act.

" . . . But I told them no thanks," Carl told Jimmy and Sheen, as they walked through the parking lot. "I'm happy to be just plain Carl."

RETROVILLE
CIVIC CENTER

Then Carl turned to his friends. "Do you think I missed dinner? For some reason, I'm craving hay."